ONCE UPON A TIME...

...On the faraway world of Eternia, twins were born to the king and queen. But soon after their birth, the little brother and sister were separated by fate.

The boy, Prince Adam, grew up on the planet Eternia. There, he learned the secrets of Castle Grayskull and that he had a great destiny. Through a magical transformation, he became He-Man, the most powerful man in the universe, and he fought on the side of goodness.

His sister, Princess Adora, was kidnapped as a baby by the wicked Hordak. She was raised by him on the planet Etheria, a world that lived in misery under the rule of Hordak and his Horde.

Only after many years were Prince Adam and Princess Adora reunited. Like Prince Adam, Adora was given a magical weapon; hers was called the Sword of Protection. Adora's Sword of Protection gave her mighty powers. With it, she was transformed into She-Ra, the Princess of Power. Her beautiful horse Spirit became Swift Wind, a flying unicorn.

Adora stayed on Etheria to work on the side of the Rebellion, which was determined to return freedom to the land. This small but dedicated band was led by Angella, queen of the Kingdom of Bright Moon.

Adora guarded the secret of She-Ra carefully. Of her many friends, only the centuries-old Madame Razz and little Kowl knew who She-Ra, the Princess of Power, really was.

One other possessed the secret of She-Ra. High atop a mountain was the Crystal Castle, a shining palace that was She-Ra's special place. At the bottom of a mysterious pool in the castle dwelled the spirit of Light Hope, She-Ra's powerful friend.

No one but She-Ra could see this wonderful castle. And only on the day that all Etheria was free would Light Hope's secrets be known to all.

It was for that day, when goodness would reign again over Etheria, that She-Ra pledged her power.

She-Ra, the Princess of Power

Written by Bryce Knorr

Illustrated by Harry J. Quinn and James Holloway

Creative Direction by Jacquelyn A. Lloyd

Design Direction by Ralph E. Eckerstrom

A GOLDEN BOOK

Western Publishing Company, Inc.
Racine, Wisconsin 53404

Library of Congress Catalog Card Number 84-062812
ISBN 0-932631-06-1
A B C D E F G H I J

Classic™ Binding U.S. Patent #4,408,780
Patented in Canada 1984.
Patents in other countries issued or pending.
R. R. Donnelley and Sons Company

"The Horde is getting closer, Mother!" Glimmer said. "Come on. We're almost to the Whispering Woods."

"I'm too tired," Angella said. "I can't keep up with you. Go on without me."

"Horde Captain Adora must not catch you," Glimmer said. She touched her staff. A flash of light shot out like an ax. It chopped down a tree and blocked the path. The Horde flyers chasing them had to stop.

Nearby, a Horde captain watched the chase. "Spring the trap," she said. "Spring it now!"

A large net fell across the path. It trapped Angella and Glimmer like butterflies.

"My wings are caught!" Angella said. "I can't get away. Go, Glimmer, before it's too late."

Glimmer gave her mother a tearful kiss. She touched her staff and disappeared.

The captain flew her Horde flyer over to Angella.
"Hello, Queen Angella," she said. "Princess Glimmer got away. But we will get you back together. After her, guards!"

A TV screen on the woman's flyer flashed to life. Hordak's face appeared. "You have done a fine job, Captain Adora," he said. "Tell Angella her rebellion is over. The Horde has captured her castle!"

On Eternia, Sorceress woke up from a spell. In front of her, a sword appeared in the air.

She tried to touch the glowing sword. But it began to move. She followed it deep inside Castle Grayskull. The sword stopped in front of one of the Doors of Mystery. Then it fell to the floor.

"Light Hope!" Sorceress said. "You found her. After all these years, we've finally found Adora!"

Sorceress brought Prince Adam to Castle Grayskull. She led him to the Door of Mystery.

"Through this door is another world," she said. "You must find someone for me. This sword will help you."

"Thanks, Sorceress," Prince Adam joked. "But I already have a sword. You gave it to me. Remember?"

"This is no time for jokes," Sorceress said. "Eternia's future is at stake. You must go to Eternia, the home of the villain Hordak."

Prince Adam stepped through the door. On the other side was a large, hollow tree in a forest.

"Help!" he heard.

A mean man chased two tiny people. Prince Adam hid behind a tree. The little people ran past him. He stuck out his foot.

"Oops," Prince Adam said when the mean-looking man tripped. "I should be more careful."

The man got up and grabbed his ray blaster.

"Trip a Horde trooper, will you?" he yelled. "I'll teach you what you should be."

  Before he could fire, a dozen rebels came out of nowhere. The Horde trooper didn't have a chance. He ran away as fast as he could.
 "Thanks for helping our friends," a young woman said. "I'm Princess Glimmer. The Rebellion could use your help."

"My name is Prince Adam," he said. "I'm from . . . er . . . a distant land. If you are against The Horde, you can count on me!"

"Good!" said another of the rebels. "I'm Bow."

"My mother is Queen Angella," Glimmer said. "Hordak has taken her prisoner on Beast Island. We must rescue her. Now where could Madame Razz be? She is supposed to help us, too."

A woman flew into the clearing on a broom. "Stop, Broom!" she yelled. The broom stopped. But the woman didn't. She flew into the air and landed safely in Prince Adam's arms.

"You are the best catch I have had in 200 years," she said.

"This is Prince Adam, Madame Razz," Glimmer said. "He's going to help us."

"As long as I don't have to fly on a broom, that is," Prince Adam said.

On Beast Island, Hordak was pleased.

"Perfect, Captain Adora," Hordak said. "Your plan is working. The rebels are almost here. We will crush their tiny rebellion!"

"Call me when you have them." Hordak got on a flyer and took off.

Captain Adora watched the rebels on her TV screen.

"Hurry up, you rebels," she said. "Why don't you get going!"

But the rebels were not going anywhere. There was no wind to push their sailboat.

"I wish we had Horde flyers," Glimmer said. "Then we could fly over the Growling Sea."

"Tut, tut!" Madame Razz said. "My magic works just as well as machines. All we need is a spell for a breeze."

Suddenly, the rebels began to *sneeze*.

"Oh my!" Razz said. "I got it wrong!"

"Your spell worked anyway," Prince Adam laughed. The rebels' sailboat was moving! They soon were far away from the shore. Then, a real breeze filled their sails.

As soon as the rebels landed on Beast Island, Adora attacked. There were many Horde troopers. All the rebels could do was run. Prince Adam started climbing toward the prison wall. But Leech cornered him.

"I'll drain your power, rebel," Leech said. Prince Adam grabbed a stick. Leech snapped at it. The stick stuck in his mouth, and Leech was helpless.

"Say ah," Prince Adam said. "Well, my friend, it looks like you have a bad case of The Horde."

Prince Adam saw a small cave nearby. He went into the cave and took out his Power Sword.

"By the Power of Grayskull," he said quickly.

"I HAVE THE POWER!"

He-Man inched his way over the wall. Only Captain Adora guarded Queen Angella.

"So *you* are Adora," He-Man said. The Horde captain jumped for a strange machine.

"I *am* Adora," she said. "And this is Hordak's Magna Beam, rebel!"

He-Man went for his Power Sword. But he grabbed Sorceress' sword instead. When he pointed the sword at Adora, it glowed with a red light.

"You are the one Sorceress wanted me to find?" He-Man asked Adora with surprise.

"You will find no one," Adora said. "This beam will take all of your power."

The Magna Beam held He-Man tight. He could not move. The sword fell to the ground.

A deep voice filled Adora's mind. "Pick up the Sword of Protection, Adora," the voice said. "It is yours."

Adora picked up the Sword of Protection. She could not stop looking at the bright glow. She didn't see the rebels climb the wall. They captured her by surprise, and she dropped the sword.

"Mother!" Glimmer cried. She untied the queen. Bow turned off the Magna Beam.

"Where is Prince Adam?" Bow asked He-Man.

"I am He-Man, his friend," He-Man answered. "I sent him on an important mission. He asked me to help you."

"What should we do with Adora?" Glimmer asked Queen Angella. "We can't leave her."

"I will guard her," He-Man said. "Please leave her with me. I must wait for Prince Adam."

"Do as you wish, He-Man," Queen Angella said. "Stay here if you like. But watch out for Captain Adora. She is as bad as Hordak!"

Queen Angella and the rebels left.

"You have great power, He-Man," Adora said. "You should join Hordak."
"But Hordak is bad," He-Man said. "Why don't you see that?"
"Hordak is not bad!" Adora cried. "Those rebels are nothing more than bandits. Hordak raised me. He gave me everything. Even my horse Spirit was Hordak's."

"You must change your mind," He-Man said. "I'm going to let you go. Take your Horde flyer. Go all over Etheria. See for yourself."

"I will, He-Man," Adora said. "But I want you to come with me. If you are wrong, you must join the Horde."

They flew all over Etheria. Adora looked closely. She saw things with new eyes. It made her very sad.

"You are right, He-Man," Adora said. "Hordak *is* bad. The people are unhappy. How could I have been so wrong? I am as bad as Hordak."

They landed her flyer by the big tree in the forest.

"I was sent here to find you, Adora," He-Man said. "I don't know why. But Sorceress would not send for someone who is bad."

"Here," he said, giving her the Sword of Protection. "This is yours."

The weapon began to glow. Two red eyes burned in its handle. Then a picture appeared.

"That's my mother! Queen Marlena of Eternia," He-Man said. "She is holding two babies."

"Prince Adam had a twin sister," a deep voice said. "A twin sister he never knew."

"Invaders from another world attacked Eternia. Hordak was their leader. Prince Adam was saved. But Horkak took the twin sister.

"That was you, Princess Adora," the deep voice continued.

The beautiful young woman could not stop staring into the Sword of Protection. She did not see He-Man step behind a tree and become Prince Adam.

"So I am Princess Adora of Eternia," she said finally. "And Prince Adam is my brother. But who is He-Man?"

"That's me," Prince Adam said. He stepped from behind a tree, raising his Power Sword.

"By the power of Grayskull," he said.

"I HAVE THE POWER!"

Adora saw Prince Adam change into He-Man. The voice from her own sword told her what to say next. She raised the Sword of Protection.

"By the *honor* of Grayskull," Adora repeated.

"I AM SHE-RA!"

Lightning flashed. Adora changed into She-Ra, the Princess of Power!

"She-Ra must fly quickly," the voice said. "Point the Sword of Protection at your horse Spirit."

Lightning flashed again. Spirit became Swift Wind, a flying unicorn!

"But who are *you*?" Adora asked the voice in the sword.

"You will find me when Castle Bright Moon is free," the voice said. "The Sword of Protection is the key. Goodbye until then."

She-Ra and He-Man heard a shout. A limb broke off the tree. Madame Razz and a funny-looking animal made a crash landing on Broom.

"Excuse us," Razz said. "We didn't mean to listen. But it's so exciting!"

"You heard everything?" He-Man asked.

"Don't worry about a thing," the animal said. "Our lips are sealed. We Kowls are very honest. And very wise."

"And very humble, too?" She-Ra asked.

"Well, Sister," He-Man said. "We have time for a quick visit to Eternia. Would you like to meet the king and queen?"

"You mean my mother and father?" Adora asked. "You bet!"

They went through the portal in the tree back to Eternia. Prince Adam took his sister into the palace through a secret entrance.

"Mother and Father don't know you are He-Man?" Princess Adora asked.

"That's right," Prince Adam replied. "Our enemies might hurt them if anyone knew. This is our parents' door. You wait here."

"Son, you're home," King Randor said. "Sorceress told us she needed you."

"Hello, Mother and Father," Prince Adam said. "I have a gift for you. A princess for Eternia!" He left to get Adora.

"A princess? For Eternia?" Queen Marlena was surprised. Her confusion changed to joy as she began to understand. "Why, a princess for Eternia could only be our long-lost daughter!"

Prince Adam led Adora through the door. Suddenly, the beautiful young woman looked very shy. The king and queen ran to hug their children.

"How can we ever thank you, Son?" King Randor asked. "Eternia's royal family is together again. Let the party begin!"

Adora was busy getting to know her home and family. But both she and Prince Adam knew that help was needed on Etheria.

"Remember what the Sword of Protection said?" Princess Adora asked her brother. "'Castle Bright Moon must be free'. And I must prove myself after all these years with The Horde. I must show that I am good. I know where to start. Don't you think the Rebellion needs She-Ra on their side?"

"You are right," Prince Adam said. "Who knows? Maybe He-Man will help you."

Princess Adora bid a tearful goodbye to her parents.

"I will come back," she promised. "But first I must help Etheria find freedom."

Princess Adora and Prince Adam went through the portal to Etheria. Madame Razz sat against the tree sleeping.

"You are back!" she said, waking up.

"I hoped we would find you," Adora said. "I'm joining the Rebellion. We have a plan to free Castle Bright Moon. Tell her, Prince Adam…"

Adora led Prince Adam to Castle Bright Moon tied up like a prisoner. Hordak was still there.

"A prisoner!" Hordak said. "You have done well again, Adora. What can I give you?"

"Only this," Adora said. She took her Sword of Protection and cut Prince Adam's ropes. "Give the castle back to Queen Angella. Stop hurting the people of Etheria!"

"You are against me, too?" Hordak shouted. He pressed a button on his arm. Alarms rang loudly. Hordak's men ran to his side. That was just what the Princess Adora wanted.

"We must hold them, Brother," Adora whispered. "I wish the rebels would get here."

"We need She-Ra," Prince Adam told her.

Adora saw a chance and went into a hallway.

"By the honor of Grayskull," she said

"I AM SHE-RA!"

She-Ra ran back to the fight just as Hordak fired. A wall fell on Prince Adam! But then Angella's soldiers rushed in. Hordak knew he could not beat She-Ra *and* the rebels. He had to run away!

"I don't know who you are," Hordak yelled at She-Ra as he ran. "But we will meet again!"

Shadow Weaver, Hordak's witch, cast a spell. The Horde disappeared!

She-Ra ran to Prince Adam. In her concern, she reached out to touch him. A golden glow covered them both. Prince Adam opened his eyes. Like magic, he was all right!

"I like having She-Ra as a sister," Prince Adam said. "You seem to have some special powers that really come in handy."

The rebels raised the flag of Bright Moon over the castle. She-Ra felt her sword starting to glow. It pointed toward a faraway mountain.

"I think my powers have something to do with that mountain," She-Ra said. "I feel drawn to it. I must go there. Want to come along?"

Prince Adam jumped onto Swift Wind. "Only if I get to fly her," he said. "Is that okay with you, Swift Wind?"

To their surprise, the unicorn talked!

"I'm glad you asked," Swift Wind said playfully. "And since you did, let's go!"

Swift Wind flew into the clouds. On top of the mountain was a beautiful shining castle.

"But how do we get in?" Prince Adam wondered.

She-Ra remembered what the voice of the Sword of Protection had said. "Of course," she said. "The Sword of Protection is the key!"

The sword unlocked the castle gate. The door slowly opened. Brother and sister walked down a winding swirl of stairs toward a dark pool. Two red eyes glowed from the bottom of the pool.

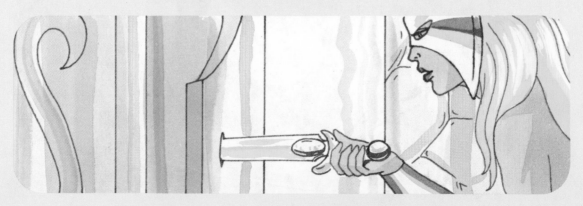

"Hello, She-Ra," a deep voice said. It was the same voice that had come from the Sword of Protection. "I am Light Hope. This is your very own Crystal Castle."

"*My* castle?" She-Ra asked.

"Yes, She-Ra," Light Hope answered. "Come here when you need help. I will be your friend.

"Only you and your brother can see this place now. But when Etheria is free, all will see its goodness."

"How long will that be, Light Hope?" She-Ra asked.

"We have many enemies," Light Hope answered. "Another already sits at Hordak's side. Her name is Catra."

A picture appeared in the pool. It showed a woman riding a large cat into The Horde's Fright Zone. The woman's beautiful face was twisted into a wicked smile.

"I know you must stay here, She-Ra," Prince Adam said. "But I must go for now. I will help you in your fight against the wickedness of Catra and Hordak whenever you need it."

"I wish you didn't have to leave," She-Ra said. "It took so long to find you. But we each have a job to do, don't we?"

   She-Ra looked down into Light Hope's dark pool. She remembered the
bad things The Horde had done. Prince Adam put his arm around his
beautiful sister.
  "Do not worry, She-Ra," Light Hope said. "You are not to blame for what
Hordak has done. You have proven your goodness. Hordak could never
take the power of goodness from you."
  "I guess everyone can be good if they want to," She-Ra said. "We just have
to make the right choices."

THE END